"So why did you jump Phelan enquired.

"Because everyone else was wearing T-shirts," replied the penguin. "And T-shirts don't have pockets, which was what I needed to hide inside to make my escape."

"Are you saying you don't want to go back to the zoo?" asked Phelan.

"Bingo!" said the penguin.

A funny, fishy tale from the talented author of *Grizzly Tales for Gruesome Kids*.

YOUNG CORGI

Young Corgi books are perfect when you are looking for great books to read on your own. They are full of exciting stories and entertaining pictures and can be tackled with confidence. There are funny books, scary books, spine-tingling stories and mysterious ones. Whatever your interests you'll find something in Young Corgi to suit you: from ponies to football, from families to ghosts. The books are written by some of the most famous and popular of today's children's authors, and by some of the best new talents, too.

Whether you read one chapter a night, or devour the whole book in one sitting, you'll love Young Corgi Books. The more you read, the more you'll want to read!

*Other Young Corgi Books to get your teeth into:*
BLACK QUEEN by Michael Morpurgo
LIZZIE ZIPMOUTH by Jacqueline Wilson
SAMMY'S SUPER SEASON by
Lindsay Camp
ANIMAL CRACKERS by Narinder Dhami

# ONE HOT PENGUIN

## Jamie Rix

Illustrated by Neal Layton

ONE HOT PENGUIN
A YOUNG CORGI BOOK : 0 552 547379

PRINTING HISTORY
Young Corgi edition published 2001

3 5 7 9 10 8 6 4 2

Copyright © Jamie Rix, 2001
Illustrations copyright © Neal Layton, 2001

The right of Jamie Rix to be identified as the author of this work has been
asserted in accordance with the Copyright, Designs and Patents Act 1988

Set in 15/19pt Bembo Schoolbook

Young Corgi Books are published by Transworld Publishers,
61–63 Uxbridge Road, London W5 5SA,
a division of The Random House Group Ltd,
in Australia by Random House Australia (Pty) Ltd,
20 Alfred Street, Milsons Point, Sydney, NSW 2061, Australia,
in New Zealand by Random House New Zealand Ltd,
18 Poland Road, Glenfield, Auckland 10, New Zealand
and in South Africa by Random House (Pty) Ltd,
Endulini, 5a Jubilee Road, Parktown 2193, South Africa

Printed and bound in Great Britain by
Cox & Wyman Ltd, Reading, Berkshire.

For Kitty and Winnie

# Contents

*Chapter One*

# THE FISH-HATER

Phelan Whelan hailed from fish stock. His father was a fisherman, *his* father was a fisherman, and *his* father was a fisherman before him. Fish, you might say, swam in the family. Until Phelan came along, that is. Phelan was only nine years old, but he knew what he didn't like.

He was a ginger-faced boy with freckles and a tangled mop of red hair cut straight across the front with pastry scissors. He had a wide-open face and a sunny smile. He was kind and generous and loved giving people presents. He lived in Ireland, in a fishing village called Ballyfishangel. And he didn't like fish.

His dad wanted his son to be a fisherman just like he was, but Phelan hated fish. He hated the feel, he hated the smell and, worst of all, he hated the taste of fish, which, on a scale of one to ten, was a twelve of a problem, because every night Phelan Whelan's mam cooked the fish that his dad had caught for supper.

His dad used to bribe him at the supper table. "If I tell you a tale of fishing, Phelan, will you not be upsetting your mother, and eat up your fish like a good boy?"

Phelan adored his dad's tales of derring-do, and enjoyed the nightly ritual in which he was told wild and wonderful sea stories to get him to eat his food.

Dad told Phelan about dragging the Irish Sea for shamrock salmon and fishing off Bondi Beach for surfboarding sharks.

He told him stories about crossing frozen oceans to the South Pole in search of Puffa whales (who wore Puffa jackets to keep themselves warm) and yeti fish, those man-eating giants of the deep, who lay in wait for passing sailors, face down in the water, pretending to be asleep. Their hairy backs made them look like floating islands of seaweed, until they sprang up and raised their toothy heads and devoured whole ships in one crunch!

Dad told Phelan tales about sailing to

the horizon and falling over the edge of the world inside a rushing waterfall that poured into a big black bucket. He told Phelan about sea monsters attacking his trawler with bolts of firewater, about flying fish with water-skis instead of feet, about mermaids and whirlpools and electric eels with sockets in the tops of their heads to allow a man to plug in his razor and shave of a morning.

While Phelan was distracted by his dad's salty tales, his mam gently spooned the fish into his mouth and Phelan ate it all without noticing. He had a powerful imagination. He only had to hear a whisper of his dad's voice to imagine himself on board the trawler, hauling up nets of schoolboy squid with inky fingers, of dogfish in kennels and catfish who purred.

But when Phelan Whelan went to bed, his mam would say to his dad: "You and your tall tales. Filling that poor boy's head with stuff and nonsense. He believes every word you say."

"Ah, there's no harm in it," his dad would say. "Would you rather I told him the truth? That I never fish further out than Puffin Island just beyond the Ballyfish Lighthouse in the Irish Sea. That fishing's a cold and wet business, and sometimes there's no fish at all. Let the boy dream, Mam. He's happy."

And Phelan Whelan *was* happy. He was a dreamer, and dreamers live with their heads in the clouds, where angels play hopscotch, and normal rules and regulations don't apply.

*Chapter Two*

# PHEW! WHAT A SCORCHER!

It was a blistering summer. The sun did not stop shining. The grass was brown, cars were dusty and rivers dried up. Phelan Whelan's mam was taking Phelan to the zoo, but Phelan wanted to wear his new green anorak.

"Are you crackers?" she cried. "It's thirty degrees out there!"

"It might rain," he said lamely, when what he really meant was, "It's my new coat, Mam. I think it looks cool and I want everyone to see it."

Fortunately his mam was too hot to argue. The temperature was tropical.

When they arrived at the zoo, Phelan's mam bought two ice creams – one for herself and one for Phelan.

The melting ice cream trickled down the cone and over the hot boy's fingers. Phelan dived in to take his first lick, but was suddenly aware that he was being watched.

He looked up and saw two polar bears and four penguins staring at his ice cream. Their sad eyes told Phelan what they were thinking. "It's so hot," they pleaded. "Give us a lick!"

Phelan was quick to oblige, but as he was sharing out his ice cream, growls, howls, bleats, cheeps, hisses and whines told him that all the other animals were hot too. He grabbed his mam's ice cream and squidged it through the hippo bars, then tugged his mam's arm and begged her (with irresistibly green eyes) to save the poor sweltering creatures.

She gave him £5, which was enough for twenty ice creams. "But that's my lot," she said. "And we'll have to *walk* home!"

The animals tried all sorts of tricks to attract the attention of the Ice Cream Kid.

Armadillos drummed on their shells, wolves sat up and begged, peacocks strutted their fantails, leopards changed their spots, elephants tap-danced, parrots quoted Shakespeare, warthogs wore false eyelashes (in a vain attempt to look pretty!) and the otters gave a spectacular display of synchronized swimming. Somehow Phelan fed them all and when he left to go home the sea lions led the animals in a grateful round of applause.

Back in the kitchen, however, when Mam removed Phelan's anorak and put it on a chair, they got the shock of their lives. The anorak moved. It wriggled and jiggled as if it was alive. It jumped off the chair and waddled across the floor.

Mam screamed while Phelan giggled. "What a wonderful thing to own," he laughed, "a walking anorak! Did you buy it from a magic shop, Mam?"

But there was nothing magic about Phelan's anorak. It ran around in circles, bumped into a table leg and fell over, revealing a dazed penguin sitting in the inside pocket.

"Afternoon," it said, in a whistling whisper of a voice that sounded like the ebb and flow of an Antarctic wind. It was a voice that only Phelan could hear. "Hot weather we're having for this time of year, wouldn't you say?"

Phelan was too startled to reply.

His mam, however, had hastily jumped to conclusions. "Phelan!" she gasped. "You wicked boy. You've stolen a penguin from the zoo!"

"I didn't steal it," protested Phelan. "It must have hitched a ride."

"And pigs can fly!" boomed his mam. Phelan made a mental note to look out for that. "You will return this poor bird to the zoo immediately."

"But—"

"But nothing, young man! Do as you're told!"

And that was that. Phelan put his anorak back on and left the house with one hot penguin in his pocket.

*Chapter Three*

# TOO HOT TO HANDLE

It was a long walk back to the zoo. Phelan and the penguin had plenty of time to chat. The penguin's name was Whistler on account of the fact that he whistled when he spoke. One day, rather stupidly, he had dived into the penguin pool without looking, only to discover that there was no water in it. He had bent his beak.

"That's this hot weather, that is," explained Phelan. "The sun's so hot it's dried up everything."

Whistler was a Gentoo penguin. He'd been born in the zoo, but had never felt at home there. His father had told him tales of a far-away land called the South Pole, where the wind blew cold off the ice floes and pricked the skin like steel pins. Whistler liked the sound of that. He wanted to live in the South Pole, where his flippers wouldn't droop in the heat.

"So why did you jump into *my* anorak?" Phelan enquired.

"Because everyone else was wearing T-shirts," replied the penguin. "And T-shirts don't have pockets, which was what I needed to hide inside to make my escape."

"Are you saying that you don't want to go back to the zoo?" asked Phelan.

"Bingo!" said the penguin. "It's too hot. From what I've heard, the penguin pool at the South Pole is as cold as a damp cave, as deep as the sky and as wide as the light from the moon."

"It's not a pool, it's an ocean," said Phelan. "The Antarctic Ocean."

"Is it?" gasped the penguin, his eyes wide with wonder. "And in this ocean, I've heard tales of fish that *swim*! Thousands of them. 'Great silver slicks of salty suppers,' my father says."

"All true," said the boy.

"So fish don't just live in buck-ets?" marvelled the bird.

Phelan smiled and shook his head.

"And rocks aren't made of plastic?"

"Only in the zoo," said the boy.

"Well I'm blowed," whistled Whistler. "I can barely believe what I'm hearing. This South Pole sounds like Paradise for penguins."

"That's exactly what it is," laughed Phelan.

There was a tiny pause while the penguin gathered his thoughts. "Phelan Whelan," he said, grinning broadly, "you've made up my mind. I'm not going back to the zoo."

"But Mam said I had to take you."

"Tell her I escaped," said Whistler. "Tell her I flew off into the sky."

"But penguins can't fly," said Phelan.

"I bet we can in the South Pole," said the penguin.

"Not even there," replied the boy. "You can toboggan on your belly though."

"Then tell her I tobogganed on my belly."

"Down the street?" snorted Phelan. "No-one can slide on concrete."

"Then tell her I'm magic!" cried Whistler desperately. He really did not want to return to the zoo.

As a general rule, Phelan Whelan did not like disobeying his mam, but had she heard how much this poor hot penguin was pining for the ice-cold ice fields of the South Pole she would have done exactly what Phelan decided to do.

"All right," he said, "I *won't* take you back to the zoo!"

The penguin gave Phelan a huge hug
and ruffled his hair with his flippers.

"Thank you," he beamed, as tears of joy splashed onto his beak. "Now if you'll excuse me, my good friend, I'd better make tracks for the South Pole." And with that the hot little penguin hopped out of Phelan's pocket and waddled off up the road. "This is the right way, I trust?"

"Stop!" called Phelan, running to catch up. "Wait! You can't just walk to the South Pole, Whistler. It's miles and miles. I've got a better idea." Phelan picked up the panting penguin and popped him back in his pocket. People in the street were starting to stare. "My dad goes fishing tomorrow, and he's *always* going to the South Pole. You could go with him."

The penguin's eyes lit up. This was an incredible piece of luck! "Your dad sails to the South Pole?"

"Yes," replied Phelan. "I'm not lying. He tells me about it every night at supper. About sailing across the frozen Antarctic Ocean, dodging Puffa whales and man-eating yeti fish!"

"Ooh, they sound scary," said Whistler. "Will you come with me?"

"No," said Phelan, "I don't go fishing. I hate fish. I hate the smell."

"Please come," begged the penguin. "I'll be scared and lonely if you don't. And how will I know when I've reached the South Pole? I'll need you there to tell me, Phelan."

How could Phelan refuse? "All right," he said reluctantly, "I'll come, but my mam's still a problem. She thinks I've put you back in the zoo. We're going to have to sneak you into the house without her knowing. That means no noise! Do we have a deal?"

31

The penguin crossed his heart and hoped to die if he so much as squawked.

Then, feeling slightly giddy, Phelan turned on his heel and ran straight back home with his secret little radiator pressed against his chest.

*Chapter Four*

# SOCK SALMON

"Did you take that hot little penguin back like I told you?" asked Mam.

"I did," lied Phelan, folding his arms across the lump inside his new anorak.

"Can I go to my room now?"

"We'll just take that coat off first."

"No!" shouted the boy. His mam drew back. "I'm cold."

"In this heat?" she gasped.

"I'm probably sick," he whimpered. "I need to go to bed, Mam."

"You're certainly acting strange," said his mam. "Maybe a rest will do you some good. I'll call you down for supp—"

But before she had finished her sentence, a very un-sick-looking Phelan had shot up the stairs and locked the door to his bedroom.

The penguin was steaming when the boy took him out of his anorak. He lay on the bed, gasping for air and pointing to his mouth for some water. "Another five minutes and I'd have been cooked," he croaked, as Phelan looked around for a mug. Unable to find one, he rushed into the bathroom with a shoe, filled it up with water and trickled the cold drink down the penguin's throat.

"Right," said Phelan. "Rules for penguins! No running. No bouncing. No hopping. No honking. No squawking. No squirming. No shuffling. No snoring. No squeaking. No fishing. No flying. No flapping. No football. And definitely no waddling to the window to wave at passers-by."

"May I breathe?" asked Whistler.

"Only if you do it quietly," ordered the boy. "Now, hide under the bed while I go down for supper and try to convince Dad that he wants to take me to the South Pole."

But before Phelan could leave, the penguin leapt off the bed, flung his flippers around the boy's neck and covered his face with kisses.

"All right!" cried Phelan. "I'll bring you some food if I can!" – which was exactly what the penguin wanted to hear.

Phelan's parents were overcome with joy. It was the first time their son had ever finished his fish supper *without* a story. What they couldn't see was that secretly, under the table, Phelan had slipped off his shoes and was posting chunks of salmon down his socks. Then, when all the fish was gone from his plate, he put his shoes back on and ate his potatoes and vegetables.

"Dad," he said, as he licked his fork clean, "can I go fishing with you tomorrow?"

His dad beamed with pride. This was the day he'd been waiting for all his life. The day his son became a fisherman. "You can," he said.

"That depends," said his mam.

"On what?" asked Phelan.

"On you continuing to eat your fish up," she said. "You're my good little boy, you are."

But Phelan did not feel good. The salmon was making his socks soggy. His toes had stuck together. "Can I leave the table now?" he asked.

"There's pudding yet," twinkled his mam. "Seeing as how you suddenly love fish, Phelan, I've got you something a tiny bit special."

Phelan's heart sank. What was it going to be? Prawn crumble with kipper custard? Octopus cake with bream cream?

"It's rice pudding," smiled his mam. Phelan heaved a sigh of relief. "With clam jam."

It tasted as horrible as it sounded but poor Phelan had to eat every last mouthful. His parents were so proud of his new-found love of fish that they couldn't take their eyes off him.

At last, Phelan squelched upstairs to bed. The taste of clam jam in his mouth turned him grey to his gills. He took off his shoes and socks, and squeezed the pulped-up fish into a soggy pile on the carpet.

"I hope those socks were clean," Whistler said warily as he sniffed at the food.

"Of course they were," said Phelan, "when I put them on – last week."

The penguin gobbled up the salmon in two greedy gulps and was just wiping his beak with his flipper when there was a knock at the door.

Phelan jumped so high his head hit the ceiling. "Into the bed!" he shrieked. "Into the bed!"

"Have you got someone in there with you?" asked his mam from outside on the landing.

"No, Mam," came the oh-so-innocent reply. "Just reminding myself to get into bed before I go to sleep."

His mam opened the door. "Are you sure you're feeling OK?" she asked.

"I wouldn't want to fall asleep on the floor, now, would I?" said the boy, throwing himself backwards across the bed to hide the penguin bump under the duvet.

"I've brought you a little treat," she said naughtily, "for being such an angel." She produced a mug from behind her back.

"Cocoa!" cried Phelan. "My favourite."

"With added chunks of chocolate squid!" she whispered wickedly.

She wouldn't leave until Phelan had drunk every last drop. Then she watched him hop under the duvet (he took great care not to kick the concealed penguin), kissed him goodnight and picked up his fishy socks. "Have I not told you enough times about taking a bath?" she sniffed, and switched off the light.

When the coast was clear and Mam's footsteps had disappeared into the kitchen, Phelan peeled back the duvet to see if the penguin was all right.

"I'm very hot and I'm still hungry!" he panted. "If I don't cool down soon my beak will droop!"

"We have to wait till Mam and Dad have gone to bed," said Phelan. "Then we can go downstairs and cool you off."

"Phew!" whistled Whistler. "Roll on the frozen South Pole!"

*Chapter Five*

# THERE'S A PENGUIN
# IN THE FREEZER

At midnight, once his parents had gone to
bed, Phelan and the hungry, hot penguin
crept downstairs
into the kitchen.
Phelan shut the
kitchen door
behind them. He
didn't want to
wake his parents.
Then he opened
the fridge door
and told the penguin to help himself.

Whistler did not need to be told twice. Ice was nice! He squeezed himself onto the middle shelf and sighed with joy as the cold gnawed deliciously into his bones. This was penguin heaven.

It was not Phelan heaven, however. No sooner had the penguin turned over to chill his belly and knocked a pot of cream onto the floor, than he buried his toes into a bowl of taramasalata and stuck his flippers into a pint of milk.

"Stop that!" Phelan cried. "Eat nicely!" But the milk bottle was already on its side and the milk was already spilt. He glanced nervously at the door, expecting his parents to appear, while the penguin stood on tip-toe and tried to push his bottom into the freezer compartment. But it was too high. The shelf collapsed under the penguin's weight and a dozen eggs exploded at Phelan's feet like yellow paint bombs. It was raining pickled herrings as the terrified boy pleaded with the penguin to stop, but the penguin wasn't listening. He was trying

to lie on top of a packet of frozen peas and was chucking out cartons of ice cream to make space.

The floor was soon covered in a chocolate-chip river of melted goo. The penguin took one look and leapt out of the fridge to do his tobogganing thing.

"Watch me slide!" he cried, as he slipped across the floor and thumped his nose on the dishwasher.

"Phelan!" came a cry from upstairs. "Is that you?"

Phelan and the penguin froze. "Yes, Dad," Phelan shouted back. "I'm just getting myself a glass of milk. There's nothing wrong!" Phelan held his breath until his father's footsteps padded back across the landing, and he heard his parents' bedroom door click shut.

The kitchen looked like the aftermath of a chimpanzees' tea party.

"That was too close!" Phelan hissed. "If my dad had come down here and seen this mess, he'd never have let us go fishing."

That brought the penguin to his senses. "You mean no South Pole?" he gasped.

"That's exactly what I mean," said Phelan, as he handed the penguin a tea towel. "So get wiping!"

By the time they had finished mopping the floor, there was a tall, crumpled pile of dirty tea towels and one penguin covered in gunk. He had egg on  his face, fish paste behind his ears and a dollop of mashed potato on the top of his head.

"You need a bath," said Phelan, as he hid the tea towels in the bread bin. "But you've got to promise not to make a noise."

Whistler promised.

So they tiptoed upstairs and Phelan ran a bath.

"Make sure it's cold," whispered Whistler, hopping onto the taps and diving in with a loud cry of, "Geronimo!"

Phelan watched in horror as the penguin's bellyflop created a tidal wave that raced the length of the bath and crashed against the wall. The noise woke up Phelan's parents again. There was a creak of bedsprings as they jumped out of bed.

"Whistler!" panicked the boy. "Stop flapping! My parents are coming. If they see you, they'll send you back to the zoo!" Mam and Dad's footsteps shuffled outside on the landing. "They're going to be so angry! We'll never go to the South Pole now!"

As the door was flung open Phelan dived into the icy bath to hide his penguin.

"What on earth are you doing?" roared his dad.

"Taking a b–b–b–bath," chattered the blue-lipped boy. "For fishy feet. Mam told me to."

"Yes, but not after midnight!" his mam cried.

"I couldn't sleep,' said Phelan.

"Are you ill?" she asked.

"I'm too excited about the fishing tomorrow," he fibbed. "I can't wait to see the South Pole."

Mam folded her arms, sighed and looked meaningfully at Dad, who looked away and said nothing. "So why have you still got your pyjamas on?" she asked.

It was such a silly question that the penguin squawked with laughter.

"What was that?" said Phelan's dad.

"A rubber duck," shouted Phelan. "I just sat on it. Could I have my towel, please?"

Phelan wrapped himself and the penguin inside the large towel and squelched back to his bedroom. Luckily his parents were so sleepy that they didn't notice the wet, webbed footprints on the carpet or the little black tail wiggling out of the bottom of the towel as Phelan shut the door.

"It's all your fault," Mam said.

"Mine!" gasped Dad.

"If you hadn't told him those silly stories about Puffa whales and yeti fish and going to the South Pole he never would have got himself so excited." Dad looked hurt. "What will you tell him tomorrow when you get to Puffin Island? The truth? That you're a million miles from the South Pole and only ten miles off the coast of Ireland?"

"I'll tell him what he wants to hear," said Dad. "If he wants it to be the South Pole, then the South Pole it shall be." Then he called out loud: "Phelan! Don't forget. Tomorrow morning. Bright and early. Wear your wellies!"

The boy and the penguin heaved a giant-sized sigh of relief. The fishing trip to freedom was still on! Then they climbed into bed and Phelan lulled his flippered friend to sleep with wild, salty tales of journeys to the South Pole, of icebergs and biting winds, and of water that was colder than a sea serpent's blood.

When Whistler went to sleep, he was smiling.

## Chapter Six

# THE ICE MAIDEN

At six o'clock the following morning a flock of noisy seagulls swooped and screeched above the trawlers that were stacked side by side in the harbour. The first

orange fingers of the sun crept over the rooftops of Ballyfishangel as Phelan and his dad walked hand in hand down the jetty towards their boat.

Phelan had a rucksack on his back. "That's got my packed lunch in it," he told his dad, when his dad tried to carry it for him. "I'd prefer to keep it on my back if you don't mind, in case I get peckish." It was only a tiny fib. He couldn't tell his dad he had a penguin in his rucksack.

Dad's trawler was huge. It had a bright red cabin and thick ropes looped across its bow. It was called the *Ice Maiden*.

"What did I tell you?" Phelan whispered to the stowaway penguin on his back. "It's got 'Ice' in its name, because my dad's always sailing to the South Pole."

"Are we nearly there yet?" asked Whistler.

"We haven't even nearly left yet!" hissed the boy.

"What was that?" said his dad.

"Nothing," came the guilty reply.

"Hoping to catch some big fish today?"

"Hoping to catch me a Puffa whale, Phelan," laughed his dad. Then he cried out, "Let her loose!" and Billy the cabin boy uncoiled the rope from its mooring. The engine fired and they slipped out of the harbour, chugging through the flat water like  a broad-beamed hippo in a swamp lake.

For the first hour Phelan's dad and Billy were busy folding nets and checking the winching gear, while the helmsman, Master Jack, held a steady course out to sea.

Phelan wandered into the wheelhouse to ask him a question. "Are we going as far as the horizon, Master Jack?"

"Aye, Phelan. That we are," came the reply.

"Isn't that a bit dangerous?" questioned the boy. "Dad's told me all about the edge of the world. What will happen if we sail over the waterfall into the bucket? I can't swim. I can float for four seconds, but I can't do strokes yet."

"We're not going that far today," laughed Master Jack. "We're only going out to Puffin Island, just beyond the Ballyfish Lighthouse."

This news came as a shock to Phelan. "*Just* beyond the Ballyfish Lighthouse?" he said. "Are you sure? I thought the South Pole was *out of sight* beyond the Ballyfish Lighthouse."

"The South Pole?" chuckled the baffled helmsman, scratching his grey beard. "Who said anything about going to the South Pole?"

Phelan's dad had forgotten to tell Master Jack of the little white lie that he'd spun to keep his son happy. And Master Jack would have gone on to  explain that Phelan's dad had never been to the South Pole in his life, had Phelan's dad not suddenly appeared with mugs of tea.

"Master Jack," he roared, "have you made the same mistake again?"

"What mistake's that?" asked the helmsman.

"When I said we were going out to Puffin Island today, did you think I meant Puffin Island just beyond the Ballyfish Lighthouse?"

"I did," said Master Jack.

"Then aren't I stupid for not making myself clear? I meant Puffin Island at the South Pole," explained Phelan's dad.

"Oh, Puffin Island at the South Pole!" exclaimed Master Jack. "Setting a course right away, skipper!" And he turned the wheel a fraction to the left and smiled at Phelan Whelan.

## Chapter Seven

# "ARE WE NEARLY THERE YET?"

A few minutes later Phelan followed his dad on deck. "Dad," he said in a worried voice, "why's it called Puffin Island?"

"Because thousands upon thousands of puffins live there," he said.

"I thought only penguins lived at the South Pole," said the boy.

"Oh no," said his dad. "Puffins too."

"As well as penguins?"

"As well as penguins, yes." Dad could see that Phelan was working something out in his head.

"And they do look alike, don't they?" Phelan asked.

"That they do," confirmed his dad.

"So some of the thousands upon thousands of puffins that live on Puffin Island might actually be penguins?" he said.

"Would that make you happy?" asked his dad.

"Because at a distance it's very easy to mistake a penguin for a puffin, isn't it?" persisted the boy.

Phelan's dad knew exactly what Phelan wanted to hear. "Now that I think of it," he said, "you're right. I *have* seen penguins on that island."

"I knew it!" shouted Phelan, slapping the rail with his hand. "So really it should be called Puffin and Penguin Island?" he said.

"If you like," smiled his dad.

Well, Phelan Whelan *did* like. He liked it very much indeed.

Just then a whistling voice whispered in the boy's ear and made him jump. "Are we nearly there yet?" it asked.

Phelan coughed to cover the penguin's
voice and ran to the other end of the boat,
where he scolded his flippered friend. "Will you
not talk to me when the others are around!"
he hissed. "They might be able to hear you."

"Sorry," said the penguin through the flap in the rucksack. "But are we nearly there yet?"

"We must be close," said Phelan, peering over the side of the boat into the dark water. "The sea's getting bigger, the wind's getting colder, and . . ." His voice trailed away till it was no more than a squeak.

"What is it?" asked the penguin.

"I've got to get my dad," whispered Phelan. He thought he'd seen a Puffa whale.

"It was!" he protested. "It was! It was under the water. It was huge and really fat."

"Are you sure it wasn't just a shadow," asked Master Jack, "and your imagination playing tricks?"

"No. It was a Puffa whale, just like in Dad's stories! It had great rolls of fat round its body like a Puffa jacket!"

"You should've said," chuckled his dad. "We could have caught it."

"Are we nearly there yet?" came the whispering voice in the rucksack.

"Will you hush!" shouted Phelan.

"I beg your pardon?" said his dad.

"Not you," stammered Phelan. "I meant the sea. Is it always this noisy or is it sometimes quiet too?" He blushed. He was making a fool of himself.

"Are we nearly there yet?" he asked quickly.

"Not far now," said his dad. "See that island in the distance?"

"Is that Puffin Island?"

"It is," said his dad.

Phelan felt the penguin give a little leap inside the rucksack.

## Chapter Eight

# TO THE SOUTH POLE

As the *Ice Maiden* chugged towards the craggy rock in the sea, Phelan's big little heart was beating nineteen to the dozen. He had never been this excited in his life. Fancy sailing all the way to the South Pole!

"It's not very far," he said suddenly. "I thought it would be further."

"That's the North Pole you're thinking of," said his dad. "That's miles and miles away. The South Pole's practically on our doorstep."

"And it's not as cold as I thought."

"It's cold enough. If you fell in that water now it'd take your breath away. Now stand out of the way, young fisherman, while Billy and I let out the nets."

Phelan stood at the front of the boat while his dad and Billy worked at the back. He opened the top of his rucksack just enough for the penguin to take a peek at his new home.

"It's beautiful," he gasped. His eyes were glistening with joy.

"It's called Puffin and Penguin Island," explained Phelan. "You're going to be so happy there. And it's not hot like the zoo, is it?"

"No," said the penguin.

"And look at that ocean," said Phelan. "I wasn't lying when I said it was big, was I?"

"It's the biggest pool I've ever seen," giggled Whistler. "I was expecting more ice though."

"That's probably because the sun's been so hot. The ice has melted. But it will come back. It's bound to. It's the South Pole."

"What's that?" the penguin asked suddenly. He lifted his head out of the rucksack and pointed his flipper at the sea.

"Where?" squinted Phelan.

"In the water over there. It's like a big black cloud."

Phelan leant forward across the rail to get a closer look. The black cloud wasn't a cloud at all. It was solid. It was made of stuff. Wild, tangled, straggly stuff, like uncombed hair; like a giant, floating bearskin rug; like the grizzled beard of King Neptune himself! Phelan's piercing scream soared above the crashing waves. "Dadaaaaaaa!"

His dad dropped his net and ran, fearing that Phelan had fallen overboard. "What is it?" he yelled, grateful to find his son safe.

"I've seen it," panted the boy, as the penguin ducked back into the rucksack.

"Seen what?" said Dad.

"The man-eating yeti fish! There, look. It's going under the boat!" The black cloud slid beneath the hull like a huge bed of floating seaweed. "Save me, Dada, save me! Don't let it eat me! Make it go away, Dada! Send it away!"

His dad put his big hand on Phelan's tiny shoulder. "It won't eat you if you don't look it in the eye," he said.

"I won't! I won't!"

"*What the yeti eye don't view, the yeti teeth don't chew!*"

Phelan's mouth was agape.

"You know what else they say?" said his dad.

"What?" gasped the wide-eyed boy.

"That a boy who sees the yeti fish on the way to the South Pole shall one day be a fisherman."

"Really?" cried Phelan. "That'd be good. What else?"

"What else?" chuckled his dad. "Have you never heard of wishing on a yeti fish?" Phelan had not. "They say that wishes made on yeti fish *always* come true."

"Gosh," gasped Phelan. Then suddenly he threw his arms around his dad's neck and kissed his cheek. "I'm just going over there," he said, pointing to the other side of the boat.

"You're no fool," said his dad. "A real wish is best made alone."

Phelan unbuckled his rucksack and lifted the penguin out.

"What did you wish for?" Whistler asked, cocking his head to one side.

"That you and me will always be friends," said Phelan softly.

"I never doubted it for a minute," he replied. "You've already been the best friend a penguin could have. You've brought me home."

The boy hugged the penguin tightly. "I'm going to miss you," he said.

"Me too," said Whistler. "But when you're a fisherman you can sail out and visit me every week."

"That I can," smiled Phelan.

"And I'll be waiting," said the penguin.

He jumped out of Phelan's arms and stood on the prow of the boat like a rather short figurehead. Then, with a smile as broad as an oyster's shell and a cry of "Geronimo!", he spread his tiny flippers, launched himself into the stinging spray and belly-flopped into the sea.

The grinning boy watched the tiny black shape as it bobbed up and down on the waves and struck out for Puffin and Penguin Island. The cold wind chiselled at his face, but Phelan Whelan felt warm to the cockles of his heart.

"Phelan!" shouted his dad. "Come and see what we've caught."

"Coming, Dad," shouted the boy, turning away from the rail and running to the back of the boat. "Is it a big fish, is it? Can I touch it, Dad, can I?"

*Chapter Nine*

# PHELAN THE FISHERMAN

When Phelan went to bed that night his head was full of fish. After only one day on the boat he had made up his mind. Like his father, and *his* father before him, and *his* father before him, he was going to be a fisherman. And when he had a boat of his own he was going to do all his fishing around a certain rock called Puffin and Penguin Island, out there in the ice-cold waters of the South Pole.

Just beyond the Ballyfish Lighthouse on an island in the middle of the Irish Sea, the

puffin-penguin
has become
something
of a local
legend. So
if ever
you're out
sailing and
happen to see a
penguin sitting on a puffin's nest, that's
Phelan Whelan's bird, that is.

And he still thinks he's living at the
South Pole, so don't you dare go telling
him different!

THE END

# DOG MAGIC!
*Chris Priestley*

*Imagine being able to wish for anything you wanted!*

Lucy has the surprise of her life when she releases a genie from an old bottle. Wow – unlimited wishes for a year! But wait a minute . . . Lucy didn't wish for dinosaur bones. And where have all the cats gone?

Why does Lucy's dog Mitch look so full of himself? *Uh-oh*. It looks like a case of dog magic!

Young Corgi books are perfect for building reading confidence.

ISBN 0 552 546887